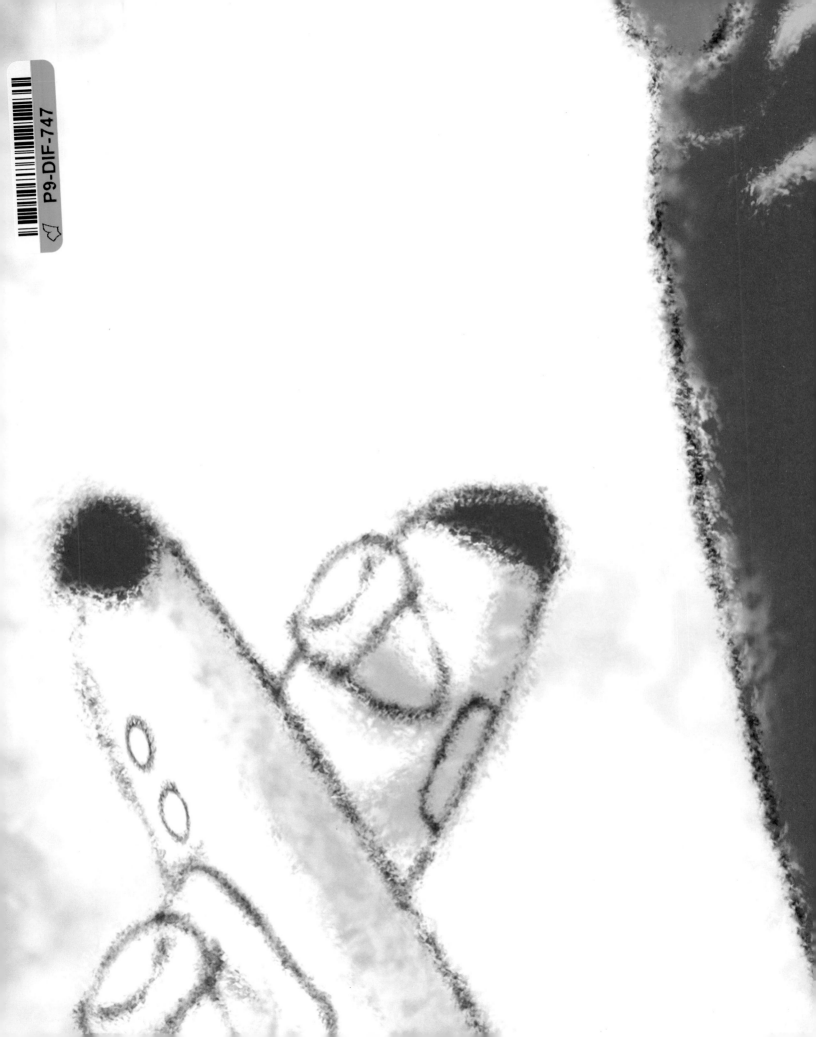

My Father FLIES

By Jennifer Guinn

Illustrated By David Kramer

Schiffer Publishing Ltd
4880 Lower Valley Road • Atglen, PA 19310

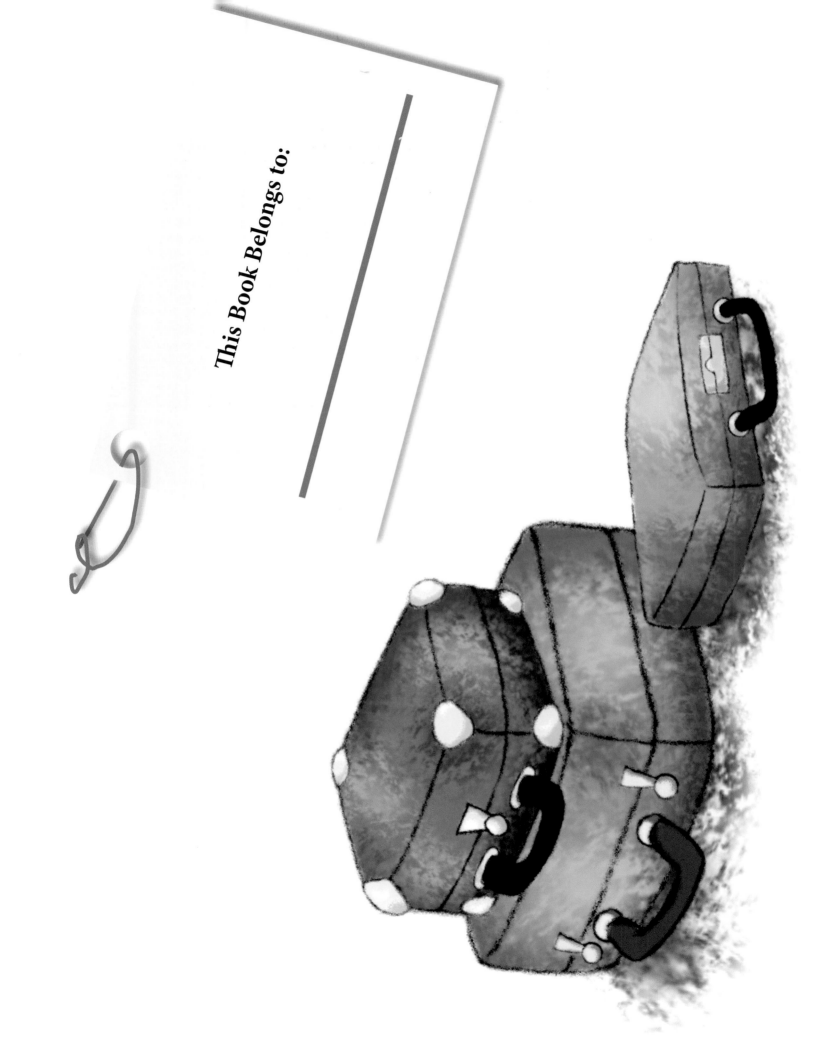

This Book Belongs to:

My father is flying through the clouds—
he's up in the sky and on his way.
And when he's halfway around the world,
he'll be in tomorrow while I'm still in today.

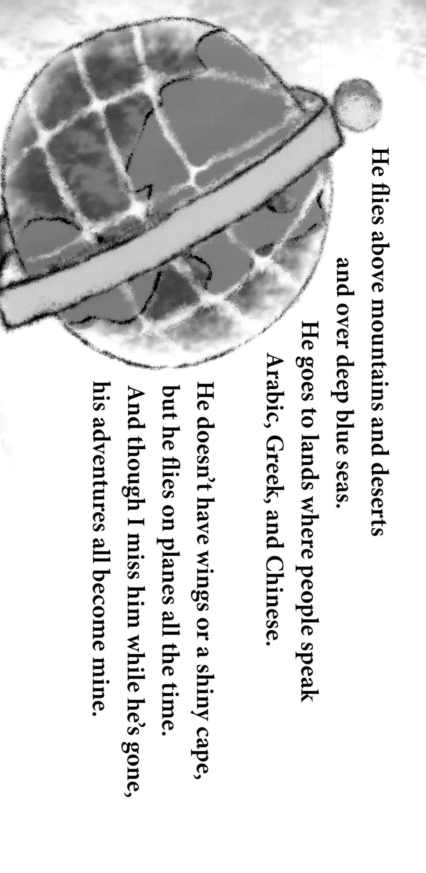

He flies above mountains and deserts
and over deep blue seas.
He goes to lands where people speak
Arabic, Greek, and Chinese.

He doesn't have wings or a shiny cape,
but he flies on planes all the time.
And though I miss him while he's gone,
his adventures all become mine.

You see,

I follow his path on my trusty globe,
my finger tracing his route.
And, one day, when I'm all grown up,
I hope to follow suit.

My dad once flew to South America,
to a country called Brazil.
He said he loved the coffee there
and the meats cooked on the grill.

But the best part of my father's trip
was when he went to a soccer game.
He said they call it *futbol* there,
but they play it just the same.

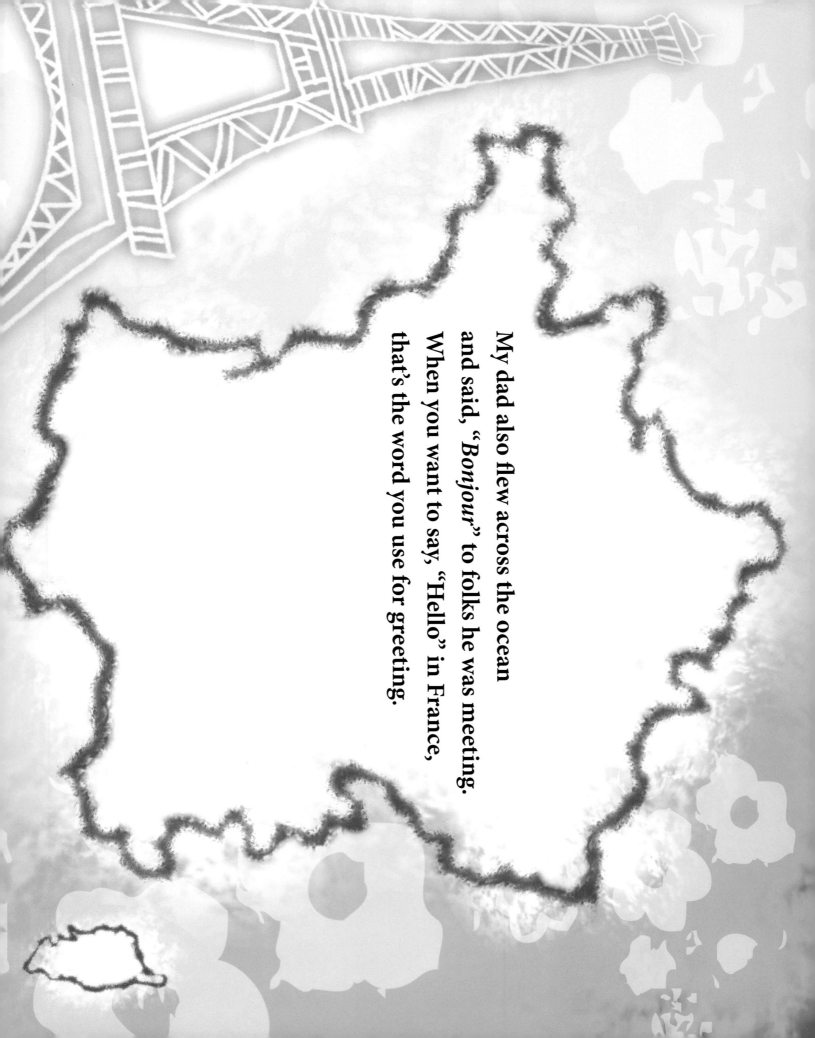

My dad also flew across the ocean
and said, *"Bonjour"* to folks he was meeting.
When you want to say, "Hello" in France,
that's the word you use for greeting.

Soon after that he visited Switzerland.
Soaring over the Alps, capped in ice and snow,
he saw cows graze on the bright green grass
in the valleys far down below.

Dad said people ski in summertime
because the mountains stay so cold,
and there are glaciers from the Ice Age
that are really, really old.

When my father came home, his suitcase was filled with the best chocolate I've ever had.

I also got a great big hug from my adventurous, globe-trotting dad.

My father then jetted further east,
to the biggest country of all.
His travels took him to a city called Moscow,
where he stopped to give us a call.

He said he tried fish eggs called caviar
when he went out to eat.
Now, I like eggs for breakfast,
but fish eggs don't sound like a treat.

He described the colorful old buildings,
how each seemed topped with a chocolate kiss.
And while there was lots to see in Russia,
it was me Dad didn't want to miss.

On his next trip, my dad flew to a land
where wild animals still roam free.
He saw lions, leopards, and hippos
when he went on a wildlife safari.

He also saw sharks and sea turtles
and a pod of big black whales.
When my dad went to Africa,
he came home with amazing tales.

My dad once flew to India,
where northern mountains stretch into the sky.
He said you could even touch the clouds,
if you hiked up really high.

Cars, scooters, motorcycles, and bikes
filled the city's busy streets.
Dad said he had some spicy dishes there,
but really loved the after-dinner sweets.

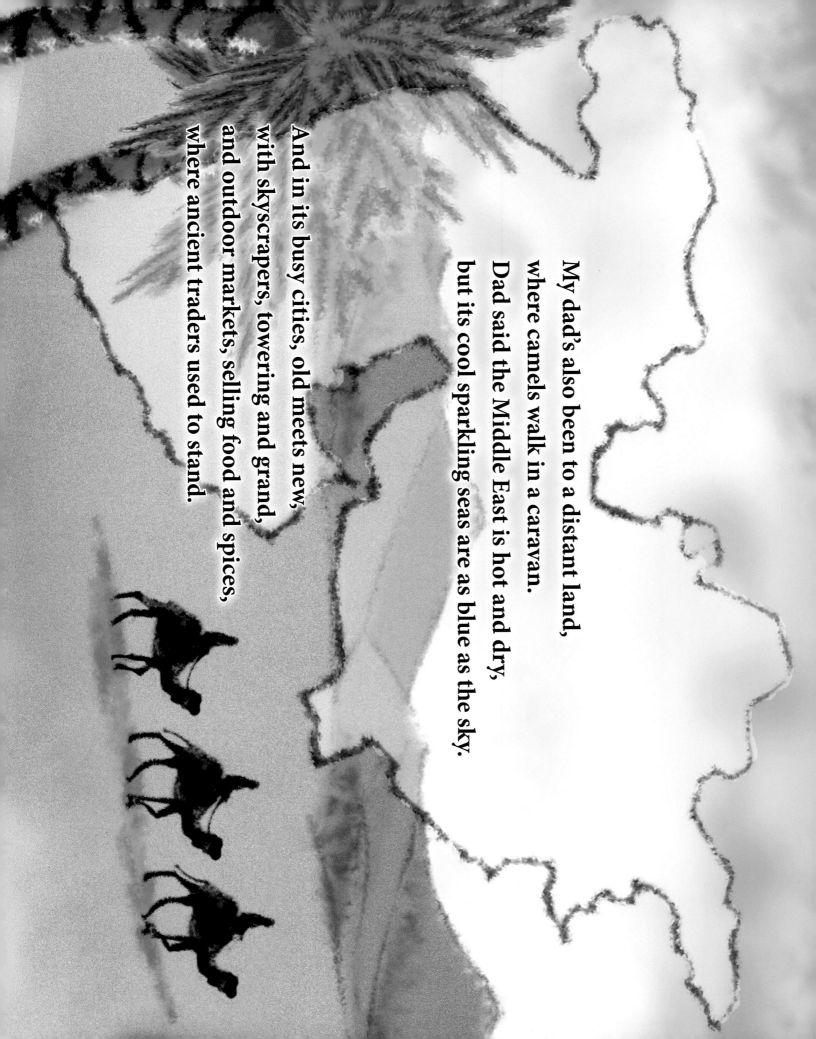

My dad's also been to a distant land,
where camels walk in a caravan.
Dad said the Middle East is hot and dry,
but its cool sparkling seas are as blue as the sky.

And in its busy cities, old meets new,
with skyscrapers, towering and grand,
and outdoor markets, selling food and spices,
where ancient traders used to stand.

Dad then went further east to Asia,

to a nation surrounded by ocean and sea.
While he was there he feasted on
rice, shrimp, and *sashimi*.

Instead of a fork, he used chopsticks to eat,
and a cushion on the floor served as his seat.
He said that there are volcanoes all over this far-away land,
which is made up of islands and called Japan.

Dad then jetted very far south
to a continent encircled by sea—
below the earth's equator,
and so very far from me.

When we talked on the phone
he said something odd about this land.
Their summer is during our winter,
which can be tough to understand.

He said the people there speak English,
but in a different way.
Instead of saying, "Hi" to friends,
Australians say, "G'day."

My dad has flown around the world
and seen amazing sights—
flying on planes and traveling
for many days and many nights.

But of all the countries he's been to
and all the places he's gone to see,
my dad says his most favorite spot
is back home here with me.

Text copyright © 2013
by Jennifer Ginn

Illustrations © 2013
by David Kramer

Library of Congress Control Number:
2012955351

Designed by Stephanie Daugherty
Type set in Minion Pro

ISBN: 978-0-7643-4385-8
Printed in China

Published by Schiffer Publishing, Ltd.
4880 Lower Valley Road
Atglen, PA 19310
Phone: (610) 593-1777; Fax: (610) 593-2002
E-mail: Info@schifferbooks.com

For our complete selection of fine books on this and related subjects, please visit our website at www.schifferbooks.com. You may also write for a free catalog.

This book may be purchased from the publisher. Please try your bookstore first.

We are always looking for people to write books on new and related subjects. If you have an idea for a book, please contact us at proposals@schifferbooks.com

Schiffer Publishing's titles are available at special discounts for bulk purchases for sales promotions or premiums. Special editions, including personalized covers, corporate imprints, and excerpts can be created in large quantities for special needs. For more information, contact the publisher.

In Europe, Schiffer books are distributed by
Bushwood Books
6 Marksbury Ave.
Kew Gardens
Surrey TW9 4JF England
Phone: 44 (0) 20 8392 8585; Fax: 44 (0) 20 8392 9876
E-mail: info@bushwoodbooks.co.uk
Website: www.bushwoodbooks.co.uk

Other Schiffer Books
by the Author:

Lobsters on the Loose,
978-0-7643-3826-7, $16.99

For my dad, the original globe-trotter,
and for my mom, who skillfully held down the fort at home

–JG

For Aidan, Grace, Isaiah, and Quinn

–DK